OF ALL POSSIBLE WORLDS

OF ALL POSSIBLE WORLDS

by William Tenn

It was a good job and Max Alben knew whom he had to thank for it—his great-grandfather.

"Good old Giovanni Albeni," he muttered as he hurried into the laboratory slightly ahead of the escorting technicians, all of them, despite the excitement of the moment, remembering to bob their heads deferentially at the half-dozen full-fleshed and hard-faced men lolling on the couches that had been set up around the time machine.

He shrugged rapidly out of his rags, as he had been instructed in the anteroom, and stepped into the housing of the enormous mechanism. This was the first time he had seen it, since he had been taught how to operate it on a dummy model, and now he stared at the great transparent coils and the susurrating energy bubble with much respect.

This machine, the pride and the hope of 2089, was something almost outside his powers of comprehension. But Max Alben knew how to run it, and he knew, roughly, what it was supposed to accomplish. He knew also that this was the first backward journey of any great duration and, being scientifically unpredictable, might well be the death of him.

"Good old Giovanni Albeni," he muttered again affectionately.

If his great-grandfather had not volunteered for the earliest time-travel experiments way back in the nineteen-seventies, back even before the Blight, it would never have been discovered that he and his seed possessed a great deal of immunity to extra-temporal blackout.

And if that had not been discovered, the ruling powers of Earth, more than a century later, would never have plucked Max Alben out of an obscure civil-service job as a relief guard at the North American Chicken Reservation to his present heroic and remunerative eminence. He would still be patrolling the barbed wire that surrounded the three white leghorn hens and two roosters—about one-sixth of the known livestock wealth of the Western

OF ALL POSSIBLE WORLDS

Hemisphere—thoroughly content with the half-pail of dried apricots he received each and every payday.

No, if his great-grandfather had not demonstrated long ago his unique capacity for remaining conscious during time travel, Max Alben would not now be shifting from foot to foot in a physics laboratory, facing the black market kings of the world and awaiting their final instructions with an uncertain and submissive grin.

*

Men like O'Hara, who controlled mushrooms, Levney, the blackberry tycoon, Sorgasso, the packaged-worm monopolist—would black marketeers of their tremendous stature so much as waste a glance on someone like Alben ordinarily, let alone confer a lifetime pension on his wife and five children of a full spoonful each of non-synthetic sugar a day?

Even if he didn't come back, his family was provided for like almost no other family on Earth. This was a damn good job and he was lucky.

Alben noticed that Abd Sadha had risen from the straight chair at the far side of the room and was approaching him with a sealed metal cylinder in one hand.

"We've decided to add a further precaution at the last moment," the old man said. "That is, the scientists have suggested it and I have—er—I have given my approval."

The last remark was added with a slight questioning note as the Secretary-General of the United Nations looked back rapidly at the black market princes on the couches behind him. Since they stared back stonily, but offered no objection, he coughed in relief and returned to Alben.

"I am sure, young man, that I don't have to go into the details of your instructions once more. You enter the time machine and go back the duration for which it has been preset, a hundred and thirteen years, to the moment after the Guided Missile of 1976 was launched. It *is* 1976, isn't it?" he asked, suddenly uncertain.

"Yes, sir," one of the technicians standing by the time machine said respectfully. "The experiment with an atomic warhead guided missile that resulted in the Blight was conducted on this site on April 18, 1976." He glanced proudly at the unemotional men on the couches, very much like a small boy after completing a recitation before visiting dignitaries from the Board of Education.

"Just so." Abd Sadha nodded. "April 18, 1976. And on this site. You see, young man, you will materialize at the very moment and on the very spot where the remote-control station handling the missile was—er—handling the missile. You will be in a superb position, a superb position, to deflect the missile in its downward course and alter human history for the better. Very much for the better. Yes."

He paused, having evidently stumbled out of his thought sequence.

"And he pulls the red switch toward him," Gomez, the dandelion-root magnate, reminded him sharply, impatiently.

"Ah, yes, the red switch. He pulls the little red switch toward him. Thank you, Mr. Gomez, thank you very much, sir. He pulls the little red switch on the green instrument panel toward him, thus preventing the error that caused the missile to explode in the Brazilian jungle and causing it, instead, to explode somewhere in the mid-Pacific, as originally planned."

The Secretary-General of the United Nations beamed. "Thus preventing the Blight, making it nonexistent, as it were, producing a present-day world in which the Blight never occurred. That is correct, is it not, gentlemen?" he asked, turning anxiously again.

*

None of the half-dozen men on couches deigned to answer him. And Alben kept his eyes deferentially in their direction, too, as he had throughout this period of last-minute instruction.

He knew who ruled his world—these stolid, well-fed men in clean garments with a minimum of patches, and where patches occurred, at least they were the color of the surrounding cloth.

OF ALL POSSIBLE WORLDS

Sadha might be Secretary-General of the United Nations, but that was still a civil-service job, only a few social notches higher than a chicken guard. His clothes were fully as ragged, fully as multi-colored, as those that Alben had stepped out of. And the gnawing in his stomach was no doubt almost as great.

"You understand, do you not, young man, that if anything goes wrong," Abd Sadha asked, his head nodding tremulously and anticipating the answer, "if anything unexpected, unprepared-for, occurs, you are not to continue with the experiment but return immediately?"

"He understands everything he has to understand," Gomez told him. "Let's get this thing moving."

The old man smiled again. "Yes. Of course, Mr. Gomez." He came up to where Alben stood in the entrance of the time machine and handed the sealed metal cylinder to him. "This is the precaution the scientists have just added. When you arrive at your destination, just before materializing, you will release it into the surrounding temporal medium. Our purpose here, as you no doubt—"

Levney sat up on his couch and snapped his fingers peremptorily. "I just heard Gomez tell you to get this thing moving, Sadha. And it isn't moving. We're busy men. We've wasted enough time."

"I was just trying to explain a crucial final fact," the Secretary-General apologized. "A fact which may be highly—"

"You've explained enough facts." Levney turned to the man inside the time machine. "Hey, fella. You. *Move!*"

Max Alben gulped and nodded violently. He darted to the rear of the machine and turned the dial which activated it.

flick!

*

It was a good job and Mac Albin knew whom he had to thank for it—his great-grandfather.

"Good old Giovanni Albeni," he laughed as he looked at the morose faces of his two colleagues. Bob Skeat and Hugo Honek had done as much as he to build the tiny time machine in the secret lab under the helicopter garage, and they were fully as eager to go, but—unfortunately for them—they were not descended from the right ancestor.

Leisurely, he unzipped the richly embroidered garment that, as the father of two children, he was privileged to wear, and wriggled into the housing of the complex little mechanism. This was hardly the first time he had seen it, since he'd been helping to build the device from the moment Honek had nodded and risen from the drafting board, and now he barely wasted a glance on the thumb-size translucent coils growing out of the almost microscopic energy bubbles which powered them.

This machine was the last hope, of 2089, even if the world of 2089, as a whole, did not know of its existence and would try to prevent its being put into operation. But it meant a lot more to Mac Albin than merely saving a world. It meant an adventurous mission with the risk of death.

"Good old Giovanni Albeni," he laughed again happily.

If his great-grandfather had not volunteered for the earliest time-travel experiments way back in the nineteen-seventies, back even before the Epidemic, it would never have been discovered that he and his seed possessed a great deal of immunity to extra-temporal blackout.

And if that had not been discovered, the Albins would not have become physicists upon the passage of the United Nations law that everyone on Earth—absolutely without exception—had to choose a branch of research science in which to specialize. In the flabby, careful, life-guarding world the Earth had become, Mac Albin would never have been reluctantly selected by his two co-workers as the one to carry the forbidden banner of dangerous experiment.

No, if his great-grandfather had not demonstrated long ago his unique capacity for remaining conscious during time travel, Mac Albin would probably be a biologist today like almost everyone else on Earth, laboriously working out dreary gene problems instead of embarking on the greatest adventure Man had known to date.

Even if he didn't come back, he had at last found a socially useful escape from genetic responsibility to humanity in general and his own family in particular. This was a damn good job and he was lucky.

"Wait a minute, Mac," Skeat said and crossed to the other side of the narrow laboratory.

*

Albin and Honek watched him stuff several sheets of paper into a small metal box which he closed without locking.

OF ALL POSSIBLE WORLDS

"You will take care of yourself, won't you, Mac?" Hugo Honek pleaded. "Any time you feel like taking an unnecessary risk, remember that Bob and I will have to stand trial if you don't come back. We might be sentenced to complete loss of professional status and spend the rest of our lives supervising robot factories."

"Oh, it won't be that bad," Albin reassured him absent-mindedly from where he lay contorted inside the time machine. He watched Skeat coming toward him with the box.

Honek shrugged his shoulders. "It might be a lot worse than even that and you know it. The disappearance of a two-time father is going to leave an awful big vacancy in the world. One-timers, like Bob and me, are all over the place; if either of us dropped out of sight, it wouldn't cause nearly as much uproar."

"But Bob and you both tried to operate the machine," Albin reminded him. "And you blacked out after a fifteen-second temporal displacement. So I'm the only chance, the only way to stop the human race from dwindling and dwindling till it hits absolute zero, like that fat old Security Council seems willing for it to do."

"Take it easy, Mac," Bob Skeat said as he handed the metal box to Albin. "The Security Council is just trying to solve the problem in their way, the conservative way: a worldwide concentration on genetics research coupled with the maximum preservation of existing human lives, especially those that have a high reproductive potential. We three disagree with them; we've been skulking down here nights to solve it *our* way, and ours is a radical approach and plenty risky. That's the reason for the metal box—trying to cover one more explosive possibility."

Albin turned it around curiously. "How?"

"I sat up all last night writing the manuscript that's inside it. Look, Mac, when you go back to the Guided Missile Experiment of 1976 and push that red switch away from you, a lot of other things are going to happen than just deflecting the missile so that it will explode in the Brazilian jungle instead of the Pacific Ocean."

"Sure. I know. If it explodes in the jungle, the Epidemic doesn't occur. No Shapiro's Mumps."

Skeat jiggled his pudgy little face impatiently. "That's not what I mean. The Epidemic doesn't occur, but something else does. A new world, a different 2089, an alternate time sequence. It'll be a world in which humanity has a better chance to survive, but it'll be one with problems of its own. Maybe tough problems. Maybe the problems will be tough enough so that they'll get the same idea we did and try to go back to the same point in time to change them."

*

Albin laughed. "That's just looking for trouble."

"Maybe it is, but that's my job. Hugo's the designer of the time machine and you're the operator, but I'm the theoretical man in this research team. It's my job to look for trouble. So, just in case, I wrote a brief history of the world from the time the missile exploded in the Pacific. It tells why ours is the worst possible of futures. It's in that box."

"What do I do with it—hand it to the guy from the alternate 2089?"

The small fat man exasperatedly hit the side of the time machine with a well-cushioned palm. "You know better. There won't be any alternate 2089 until you push that red switch on the green instrument panel. The moment you do, our world, with all its slow slide to extinction, goes out and its alternate goes on—just like two electric light bulbs on a push-pull circuit. We and every single one of our artifacts, including the time machine, disappear. The problem is how to keep that manuscript from disappearing.

"Well, all you do, if I have this figured right, is shove the metal box containing the manuscript out into the surrounding temporal medium a moment before you materialize to do your job. That temporal medium in which you'll be traveling is something that exists independent of and autonomous to all possible futures. It's my hunch that something that's immersed in it will not be altered by a new time sequence."

*

"Remind him to be careful, Bob," Honek rumbled. "He thinks he's Captain Blood and this is his big chance to run away to sea and become a swashbuckling pirate."

Albin grimaced in annoyance. "I *am* excited by doing something besides sitting in a safe little corner working out safe little abstractions for the first time in my life. But I know that this is a first experiment. Honestly, Hugo, I really have enough intelligence to recognize that simple fact. I know that

11

if anything unexpected pops up, anything we didn't foresee, I'm supposed to come scuttling back and ask for advice."

"I hope you do," Bob Skeat sighed. "I hope you do know that. A twentieth century poet once wrote something to the effect that the world will end not with a bang, but a whimper. Well, our world is ending with a whimper. Try to see that it doesn't end with a bang, either."

"That I'll promise you," Albin said a trifle disgustedly. "It'll end with neither a bang *nor* a whimper. So long, Hugo. So long, Bob."

He twisted around, reaching overhead for the lever which activated the forces that drove the time machine.

flick!

*

It was strange, Max Alben reflected, that this time travel business, which knocked unconscious everyone who tried it, only made him feel slightly dizzy. That was because he was descended from Giovanni Albeni, he had been told. There must be some complicated scientific explanation for it, he decided—and that would make it none of his business. Better forget about it.

All around the time machine, there was a heavy gray murk in which objects were hinted at rather than stated definitely. It reminded him of patrolling his beat at the North American Chicken Reservation in a thick fog.

According to his gauges, he was now in 1976. He cut speed until he hit the last day of April, then cut speed again, drifting slowly backward to the eighteenth, the day of the infamous Guided Missile Experiment. Carefully, carefully, like a man handling a strange bomb made on a strange planet, he watched the center gauge until the needle came to rest against the thin etched line that indicated the exactly crucial moment. Then he pulled the brake and stopped the machine dead.

All he had to do now was materialize in the right spot, flash out and pull the red switch toward him. Then his well-paid assignment would be done. But....

He stopped and scratched his dirt-matted hair. Wasn't there something he was supposed to do a second before materialization? Yes, that useless old windbag, Sadha, had given him a last instruction.

WILLIAM TENN

He picked up the sealed metal cylinder, walked to the entrance of the time machine and tossed it into the gray murk. A solid object floating near the entrance caught his eye. He put his arm out—whew, it was cold!—and pulled it inside.

A small metal box. Funny. What was it doing out there? Curiously, he opened it, hoping to find something valuable. Nothing but a few sheets of paper, Alben noted disappointedly. He began to read them slowly, very slowly, for the manuscript was full of a lot of long and complicated words, like a letter from one bookworm scientist to another.

The problems all began with the Guided Missile Experiment of 1976, he read. There had been a number of such experiments, but it was the one of 1976 that finally did the damage the biologists had been warning about. The missile with its deadly warhead exploded in the Pacific Ocean as planned, the physicists and the military men went home to study their notes, and the world shivered once more over the approaching war and tried to forget about it.

But there was fallout, a radioactive rain several hundred miles to the north, and a small fishing fleet got thoroughly soaked by it. Fortunately, the radioactivity in the rain was sufficiently low to do little obvious physical damage: All it did was cause a mutation in the mumps virus that several of the men in the fleet were incubating at the time, having caught it from the children of the fishing town, among whom a minor epidemic was raging.

*

The fleet returned to its home town, which promptly came down with the new kind of mumps. Dr. Llewellyn Shapiro, the only physician in town, was the first man to note that, while the symptoms of this disease were substantially milder than those of its unmutated parent, practically no one was immune to it and its effects on human reproductivity were truly terrible. Most people were completely sterilized by it. The rest were rendered much less capable of fathering or bearing offspring.

Shapiro's Mumps spread over the entire planet in the next few decades. It leaped across every quarantine erected; for a long time, it successfully defied all the vaccines and serums attempted against it. Then, when a vaccine was finally perfected, humanity discovered to its dismay that its generative powers had been permanently and fundamentally impaired.

13

UF ALL POSSIBLE WORLDS

Something had happened to the germ plasm. A large percentage of individuals were born sterile, and, of those who were not, one child was usually the most that could be expected, a two-child parent being quite rare and a three-child parent almost unknown.

Strict eugenic control was instituted by the Security Council of the United Nations so that fertile men and women would not be wasted upon non-fertile mates. Fertility was the most important avenue to social status, and right after it came successful genetic research.

Genetic research had the very best minds prodded into it; the lesser ones went into the other sciences. Everyone on Earth was engaged in some form of scientific research to some extent. Since the population was now so limited in proportion to the great resources available, all physical labor had long been done by robots. The government saw to it that everybody had an ample supply of goods and, in return, asked only that they experiment without any risk to their own lives—every human being was now a much-prized, highly guarded rarity.

There were less than a hundred thousand of them, well below the danger point, it had been estimated, where a species might be wiped out by a new calamity. Not that another calamity would be needed. Since the end of the Epidemic, the birth rate had been moving further and further behind the death rate. In another century....

That was why a desperate and secret attempt to alter the past was being made. This kind of world was evidently impossible.

Max Alben finished the manuscript and sighed. What a wonderful world! What a comfortable place to live!

He walked to the rear dials and began the process of materializing at the crucial moment on April 18, 1976.

flick!

*

It was odd, Mac Albin reflected, that these temporal journeys, which induced coma in everyone who tried it, only made him feel slightly dizzy. That was because he was descended from Giovanni Albeni, he knew. Maybe there was some genetic relationship with his above-average fertility—might be a good idea to mention the idea to a biologist or two when he returned. *If* he returned.

WILLIAM TENN

All around the time machine, there was a soupy gray murk in which objects were hinted at rather than stated definitely. It reminded him of the problems of landing a helicopter in a thick fog when the robot butler had not been told to turn on the ground lights.

According to the insulated register, he was now in 1976. He lowered speed until he registered April, then maneuvered slowly backward through time to the eighteenth, the day of the infamous Guided Missile Experiment. Carefully, carefully, like an obstetrician supervising surgical robots at an unusually difficult birth, he watched the register until it rolled to rest against the notch that indicated the exactly crucial moment. Then he pushed a button and froze the machine where it was.

All he had to do now was materialize in the right spot, flash out and push the red switch from him. Then his exciting adventure would be over.

But....

He paused and tapped at his sleek chin. He was supposed to do something a second before materialization. Yes, that nervous theoretician, Bob Skeat, had given him a last suggestion.

He picked up the small metal box, twisted around to face the opening of the time machine and dropped it into the gray murk. A solid object floating near the opening attracted his attention. He shot his arm out—it was *cold*, as cold as they had figured—and pulled the object inside.

A sealed metal cylinder. Strange. What was it doing out there? Anxiously, he opened it, not daring to believe he'd find a document inside. Yes, that was exactly what it was, he saw excitedly. He began to read it rapidly, very rapidly, as if it were a newly published paper on neutrinos. Besides, the manuscript was written with almost painful simplicity, like a textbook composed by a stuffy pedagogue for the use of morons.

The problems all began with the Guided Missile Experiment of 1976, he read. There had been a number of such experiments, but it was the one of 1976 that finally did the damage the biologists had been warning about. The missile with its deadly warhead exploded in the Brazilian jungle through some absolutely unforgivable error in the remote-control station, the officer in charge of the station was reprimanded and the men under him court-martialed, and the Brazilian government was paid a handsome compensation for the damage.

*

OF ALL POSSIBLE WORLDS

But there had been more damage than anyone knew at the time. A plant virus, similar to the tobacco mosaic, had mutated under the impact of radioactivity. Five years later, it burst out of the jungle and completely wiped out every last rice plant on Earth. Japan and a large part of Asia became semi-deserts inhabited by a few struggling nomads.

Then the virus adjusted to wheat and corn—and famine howled in every street of the planet. All attempts by botanists to control the Blight failed because of the swiftness of its onslaught. And after it had fed, it hit again at a new plant and another and another.

Most of the world's non-human mammals had been slaughtered for food long before they could starve to death. Many insects, too, before they became extinct at the loss of their edible plants, served to assuage hunger to some small extent.

But the nutritive potential of Earth was steadily diminishing in a horrifying geometric progression. Recently, it had been observed, plankton—the tiny organism on which most of the sea's ecology was based—had started to disappear, and with its diminution, dead fish had begun to pile up on the beaches.

Mankind had lunged out desperately in all directions in an effort to survive, but nothing had worked for any length of time. Even the other planets of the Solar System, which had been reached and explored at a tremendous cost in remaining resources, had yielded no edible vegetation. Synthetics had failed to fill the prodigious gap.

In the midst of the sharply increasing hunger, social controls had pretty much dissolved. Pathetic attempts at rationing still continued, but black markets became the only markets, and black marketeers the barons of life. Starvation took the hindmost, and only the most agile economically lived in comparative comfort. Law and order were had only by those who could afford to pay for them and children of impoverished families were sold on the open market for a bit of food.

But the Blight was still adjusting to new plants and the food supply kept shrinking. In another century....

That was why the planet's powerful individuals had been persuaded to pool their wealth in a desperate attempt to alter the past. This kind of world was manifestly impossible.

WILLIAM TENN

Mac Albin finished the document and sighed. What a magnificent world! What an exciting place to live!

He dropped his hand on the side levers and began the process of materializing at the crucial moment on April 18, 1976.

flick!

*

As the equipment of the remote-control station began to take on a blurred reality all around him, Max Alben felt a bit of fear at what he was doing. The technicians, he remembered, the Secretary-General, even the black market kings, had all warned him not to go ahead with his instructions if anything unusual turned up. That was an awful lot of power to disobey: he knew he should return with this new information and let better minds work on it.

They with their easy lives, what did they know what existence had been like for such as he? Hunger, always hunger, scrabbling, servility, and more hunger. Every time things got really tight, you and your wife looking sideways at your kids and wondering which of them would bring the best price. Buying security for them, as he was now, at the risk of his life.

But in this other world, this other 2089, there was a state that took care of you and that treasured your children. A man like himself, with *five* children—why, he'd be a big man, maybe the biggest man on Earth! And he'd have robots to work for him and lots of food. Above all, lots and lots of food.

He'd even be a scientist—*everyone* was a scientist there, weren't they?—and he'd have a big laboratory all to himself. This other world had its troubles, but it was a lot nicer place than where he'd come from. He wouldn't return. He'd go through with it.

The fear left him and, for the first time in his life, Max Alben felt the sensation of power.

He materialized the time machine around the green instrument panel, sweating a bit at the sight of the roomful of military figures, despite the technicians' reassurances that all this would be happening too fast to be visible. He saw the single red switch pointing upward on the instrument panel. The switch that controlled the course of the missile. Now! Now to make a halfway decent world!

Max Alben pulled the little red switch toward him.

OF ALL POSSIBLE WORLDS

*

As the equipment of the remote-control station began to oscillate into reality all around him, Mac Albin felt a bit of shame at what he was doing. He'd promised Bob and Hugo to drop the experiment at any stage if a new factor showed up. He knew he should go back with this new information and have all three of them kick it around.

But what would they be able to tell him, they with their blissful adjustment to their thoroughly blueprinted lives? They, at least, had been ordered to marry women they could live with; he'd drawn a female with whom he was completely incompatible in any but a genetic sense. Genetics! He was tired of genetics and the sanctity of human life, tired to the tip of his uncalloused fingers, tired to the recesses of his unused muscles. He was tired of having to undertake a simple adventure like a thief in the night.

But in this other world, this other 2089, someone like himself would be a monarch of the black market, a suzerain of chaos, making his own rules, taking his own women. So what if the weaklings, those unfit to carry on the race, went to the wall? His kind wouldn't.

He'd formed a pretty good idea of the kind of men who ruled that other world, from the document in the sealed metal cylinder. The black marketeers had not even read it. Why, the fools had obviously been duped by the technicians into permitting the experiment; they had not grasped the idea that an alternate time track would mean their own non-existence.

This other world had its troubles, but it was certainly a livelier place than where he'd come from. It deserved a chance. Yes, that was how he felt: his world was drowsily moribund; this alternate was starving but managing to flail away at destiny. It *deserved* a chance.

Albin decided that he was experiencing renunciation and felt proud.

He materialized the time machine around the green instrument panel, disregarding the roomful of military figures since he knew they could not see him. The single red switch pointed downward on the instrument panel. That was the gimmick that controlled the course of the missile. Now! Now to make a halfway interesting world!

Mac Albin pushed the little red switch from him.

flick!

18

WILLIAM TENN

Now! Now to make a halfway decent world!
Max Alben pulled the little red switch toward him.

   flick!

Now! Now to make a halfway interesting world!
Mac Albin pushed the little red switch from him.

   flick!

... pulled the little red switch toward him.

   flick!

... pushed the little red switch from him.

   flick!

... toward him.

   flick!

... from him.

   flick!